Rumble's Happy Wiggle

Lisa Marie Johnson

ISBN 978-1-0980-8366-3 (paperback)
ISBN 978-1-0980-8367-0 (hardcover)
ISBN 978-1-0980-8368-7 (digital)

Christian Faith Publishing, Inc.
832 Park Avenue
Meadville, PA 16335
www.christianfaithpublishing.com

Printed in the United States of America

In loving memory of the best dog ever!

Rumble, you were taken from us way to early, and it

breaks our hearts every day we don't get to love on you.

We are so very thankful for the time we had with you.

You impacted our lives in such an amazing way.

We will never forget you, buddy. You taught us to

love even deeper than we ever thought possible.

RIP, big Rumble boy.

We love you.

Rumble is a Rottweiler.

Rumble's curiosity is always getting him in trouble.

Rumble likes to get in the trash cans.

Rumble sometimes drinks from the toilet.

Sometimes Rumble doesn't listen well. We took Rumble to the animal doctor to get his ears checked. But Rumble was just being stubborn.

One morning, Rumble woke early, ate his breakfast, and headed out for a walk. On his walk, he came across some ducks at the nearby pond.

Rumble loved being outside. He could stay outside for hours just smelling the air and listening to the wind. Rumble lay in the grass in the sun for about an hour; he hardly moved. The birds were singing, the wind was blowing, and little bugs were flying by, checking out the large dog relaxing in the sun.

The sky was beautiful, and the water was unusually clear. Rumble could see the fish swimming in the water. He tried to catch the fish. He tried to chase the ducks.

He ended up all alone at the pond. All the wildlife disappeared. Rumble was sad that all the animals left him. He didn't mean to chase them away; he just wanted to play.

Rumble thought to himself and tried to figure out how to not scare the animals away next time. He loved seeing the animals. Rumble loved playing with the animals. However, his size and eagerness chased everyone away.

Rumble went home that afternoon sad, and he tried to think of a new plan for the next day.

That evening, as Rumble went to bed, he dreamed of all the fun he would have the next day at the nearby pond.

Rumble woke extra early, but he couldn't forget his favorite part of the day—breakfast. Well, actually, breakfast, lunch, and dinner were his favorite parts of the day. Rumble loves to eat!

Rumble ran down to the pond.

All the animals were there: ducks, geese, fish, and even a couple deer. Rumble was very careful this time. He walked to the water line and rolled over onto his back and did a very happy wiggle.

While upside down, he wiggled back and forth. This made Rumble so happy! The fish watched Rumble, and the ducks watched while the geese came a little closer. They were very interested in Rumble's fun moves.

Rumble was having so much fun! The other animals decided to join in. They flipped around and wiggled on the grass.

The ducks quacked in excitement.

The fish jumped and splashed.

The deer, happy, wiggled from the other side of the pond.

Even the birds in the trees chirped and sang along with the fun.

This made Rumble so happy!

All the fun lasted for hours. The animals were so tired at the end of the day.

Rumbled walked home with a joy in his heart and a skip in his step.

When Rumble lay down to go to bed that night, he was very happy. His happy wiggle made all the wildlife happy too.

Rumble continued to go to the pond every single day and do his happy wiggle for the animals. This made everyone smile.

Just one simple action brought so much joy to everyone.

CPSIA information can be obtained
at www.ICGtesting.com
Printed in the USA
BVHW092356070421
604337BV00022B/2900